I Am a Rock

by Jean Marzollo
Illustrated by Judith Moffatt

Hello Reader! Science — Level 1

Cartwheel
·B·O·O·K·S·®

SCHOLASTIC INC.

New York   Toronto   London   Auckland   Sydney

Hello, Family Members,

Learning to read is one of the most important accomplishments of early childhood. **Hello Reader!** books are designed to help children become skilled readers who like to read. Beginning readers learn to read by remembering frequently used words like "the," "is," and "and"; by using phonics skills to decode new words; and by interpreting picture and text clues. These books provide both the stories children enjoy and the structure they need to read fluently and independently. Here are suggestions for helping your child *before*, *during*, and *after* reading:

Before

- Look at the cover and pictures and have your child predict what the story is about.
- Read the story to your child.
- Encourage your child to chime in with familiar words and phrases.
- Echo read with your child by reading a line first and having your child read it after you do.

During

- Have your child think about a word he or she does not recognize right away. Provide hints such as "Let's see if we know the sounds" and "Have we read other words like this one?"
- Encourage your child to use phonics skills to sound out new words.
- Provide the word for your child when more assistance is needed so that he or she does not struggle and the experience of reading with you is a positive one.
- Encourage your child to have fun by reading with a lot of expression . . . like an actor!

After

- Have your child keep lists of interesting and favorite words.
- Encourage your child to read the books over and over again. Have him or her read to brothers, sisters, grandparents, and even teddy bears. Repeated readings develop confidence in young readers.
- Talk about the stories. Ask and answer questions. Share ideas about the funniest and most interesting characters and events in the stories.

I do hope that you and your child enjoy this book.

—Francie Alexander
Reading Specialist,
Scholastic's Instructional Publishing Group

If you have questions or comments about how children learn to read, please contact Francie Alexander at FrancieAl@aol.com

For Claudio, my rock
— J. Marzollo

To my rockin' *friends:*
Katy, Chris, and Zach
— J. Moffatt

The editors would like to thank Margaret Carruthers
of the American Museum of Natural History,
New York, for her expertise.

Cut-paper photography by Paul Dyer.

Photographs of rock samples on pages 30-31 as follows: Chalk and flint
samples, Breck P. Kent, photographer. Iron sample courtesy of B. Walsh,
J. Beckett, and M. Carruthers. All other rock samples supplied by Photo
Researchers — photographers: granite, Andrew J. Martinez; salt, François
Gohier; gold, Dan Suzio; sandstone, Joyce Photograghics; slate, Aaron Haupt;
diamond, Charles D. Winters; talc, Ben Johnson/Science Photo Library; coal,
Geoff Lane/CSIRO/Science Photo Library; petrified wood, Jim Steinberg.

Library of Congress Cataloging-in-Publication Data

Marzollo, Jean.
    I am a rock / by Jean Marzollo; illustrated by Judith Moffatt.
       p.   cm. — (Hello reader! Level 1)
    Summary: First - person riddles present information about various rocks
and minerals, including sandstone, chalk, slate, and petrified wood.
    ISBN 0-590-37222-X
    1. Rocks — Juvenile literature.   2. Minerals—Juvenile literature.
[1. Rocks — Miscellanea.   2. Minerals—Miscellanea.   3. Questions and
answers.]   I. Moffatt, Judith, ill.   II. Title.   III. Series.
QE432.2.M287 1998
552 — dc21
                                        97-16373
                                            CIP
                                            AC

12 11 10 9 8 7 6 5 4 3 2 1   8 9/9 0/0 01 02

Printed in the U.S.A.   24
First printing, February 1998

Welcome to the
Rock Hall of Fame.
My name is Marble.
Come and meet
my friends.
Can you tell
who they are?

I am a famous granite rock.
The Pilgrims stepped on me
when they came to America.
Who am I?

Plymouth Rock

I am white and tasty.
You can sprinkle me
on your food.
Who am I?

Salt

I am used for money
and jewelry.
Who am I?

Gold

I am melted
to make glass.
Glassblowers make
shapes from me.
Who am I?

Sandstone

You can write with me.
You can draw with me.
Who am I?

Chalk

I am flat enough to walk on.
I am flat enough to write on.
Who am I?

Slate

I dazzle! I sparkle!
I am a jewel!
I am also very hard.
People use me to cut glass.
Who am I?

Diamond

I am ground into powder.
People can shake me on
babies to keep them dry.
Who am I?

Talc

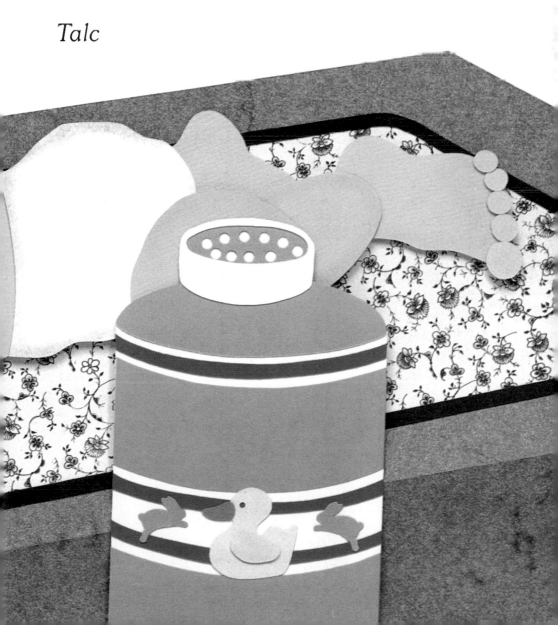

I hold heat well. People use me to make frying pans and wood-burning stoves. If I get wet, I rust. Who am I?

Iron

Strike me against a rock.
See the spark?
Campers can use me
to start fires.
Who am I?

Flint

I burn slowly.
People can use me
for heat and power.
Who am I?

Coal

I look like wood.
I used to *be* wood.
But I am not wood anymore.
Who am I?

Petrified wood

Rocks: Facts and Photos

Rocks are on the ground.
Rocks are under the ground.

Granite

Salt

Gold

Sandstone

Chalk

Slate

Rocks are made of minerals.
Rocks are everywhere on earth.

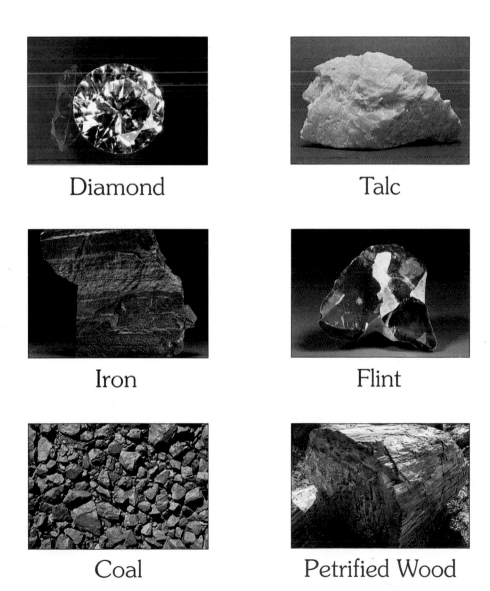

Diamond

Talc

Iron

Flint

Coal

Petrified Wood

Thank you for coming
to the Rock Hall of Fame!
Good-bye.